This is the story of three little pigs,

and houses built of straw, bricks, twigs.

There's something else.

Can you guess what?

On every page there's a pot to spot!

Three
Little Pigs

Illustrations by Katie Saunders

make
believe
ideas

One day, three little pigs
pack their bags.
They wave good-bye
to their mother.

Sale
50% off

The first little pig builds
a house out of straw.
Mr Wolf is watching him!

The second little pig builds
a house out of wood.
Mr Wolf is watching him!

25% off

Edward
Woodwood
Supplies

Edward
Woodwood
Supplies

The third little pig builds
a house out of bricks.
Mr Wolf is watching him!

14

"I am hungry!"
says Mr Wolf.

Houses from Straw

"Let me in!"
says Mr Wolf,
"or I will blow
your house down!"

"Let me in!"
says Mr Wolf,
"or I will blow
your house down!"

19

Mr Wolf climbs up
the brick house.

No Salesmen
No Wolves
Please!

No Wolves

21

Mr Wolf jumps
down the chimney.

He falls into a
pot of hot water.
"Ouch!" he shouts.

Mr Wolf runs away.
The three little pigs
live happily ever after
in the house of bricks.

Ready to tell

Oh no! Some of the pictures from this story have been mixed up! Can you retell the story and point to each picture in the correct order?

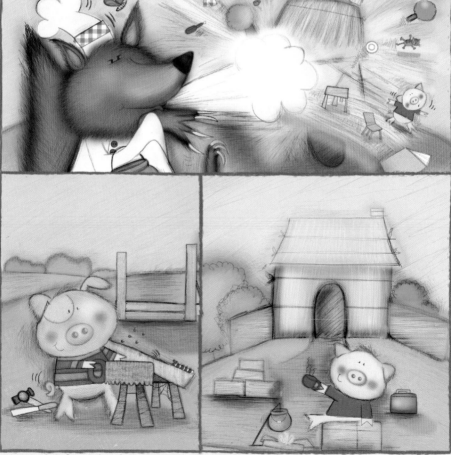

Picture dictionary

Encourage your child to read these words from the story and gradually develop his or her basic vocabulary.

bricks

builds

chimney

climbs

house

pot

straw

wolf

wood

Key words

Here are some key words used in context. Help your child to use other words from the border in simple sentences.

The three little pigs pack their bags.

The pig builds a house out **of** wood.

"**I** will blow your house down!" says Mr Wolf.

Mr Wolf falls into **a** pot of hot water.

Mr Wolf runs **away**.

Build a house

The three little pigs were good at building houses. Now it's your turn—here's how!

You will need

3 small cardboard boxes • scissors • glue • felt-tip marker • paper • cardboard • straw • twigs • paint • sponge

What to do

1 Cover each box with paper and glue it on.
2 Use the marker to draw a door and windows. Ask a grown-up to help you cut them out.
3 Glue the straw or twigs onto the sides of two of the boxes. For the brick house, cut a small rectangle of sponge and apply paint. Then stamp rows of bricks on the walls.
4 To make the roof, cut a rectangle out of cardboard and fold it down the middle. Glue on your chosen covering. Put glue on the top edges of your box and carefully attach the roof.

Hints and tips

• If you don't have straw, try using packing material, raffia, yellow tissue or crêpe paper twisted into strips.
• Use popsicle sticks or toothpicks instead of twigs.
• Make a garden with trees made from pinecones and pigs made from corks!